THE HORSEMAN'S SEED

SEED

A KILLER'S APPRENTICE

PLAYSCRIPT

GUY SAULS

For Catherine

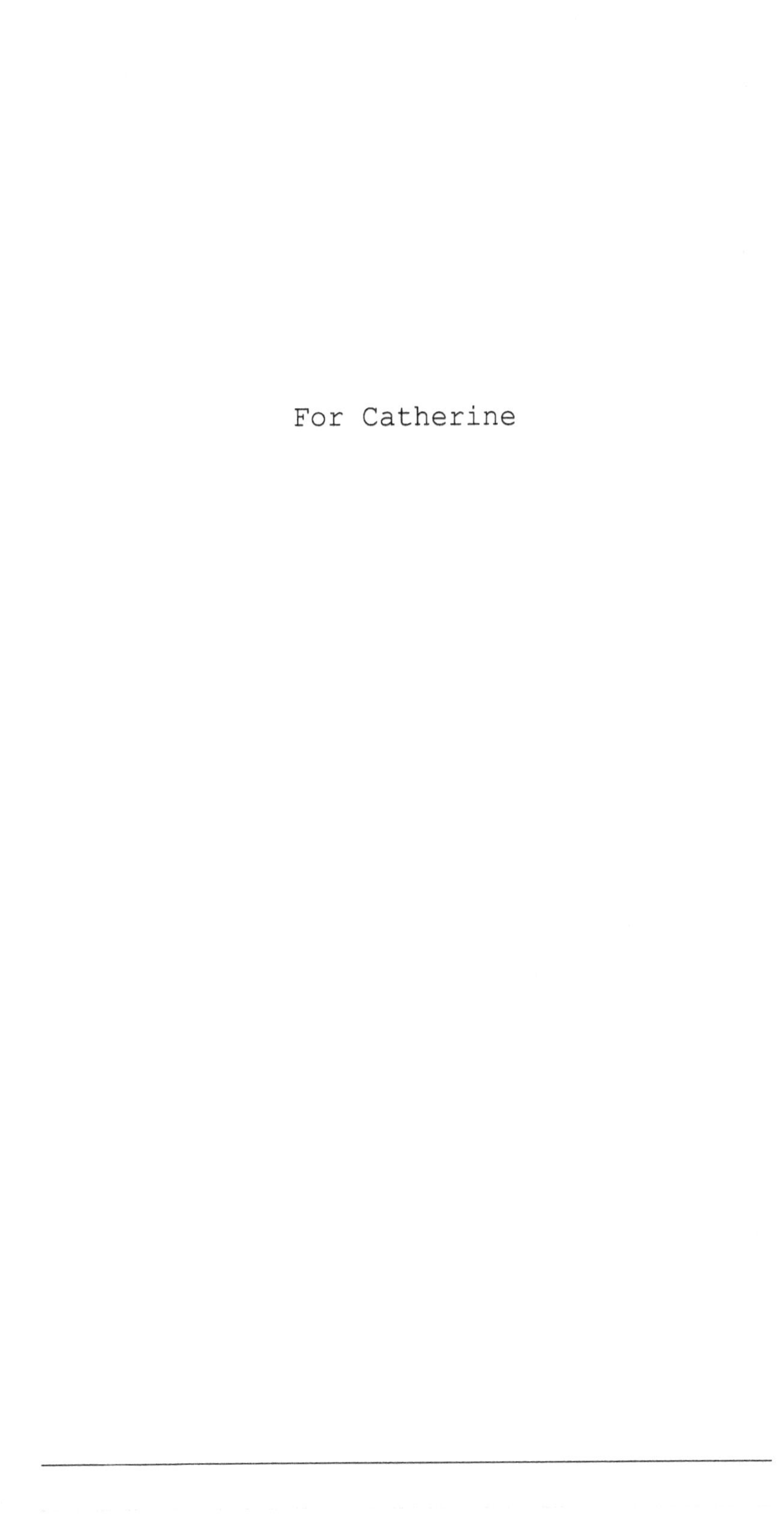

CHARACTER DESCRIPTIONS

JOHN
    Kindhearted and slightly slow-witted
    with an occasional speech impediment
    suffering from PTSD. Role matures
    from AGE 14 to 55. A different actor
    may play AGE 14.

NANCY
    Professional psychiatrist with a
    sympathetic ear and straightforward
    approach.

SAM
    Muscular, attractive, manipulative,
    and aggressively sociopathic.

HIM
    Faceless and dressed in black. Grim
    reaper style. HIM is a demon in
    John's mind.

SEAN
    Athletic. Role matures from AGE 17 to
    a 35-year-old NFL star.

ABAGAIL
    A mature elderly loving woman.
    ABAGAIL is an angel in John's mind.

SHARON
    John's middle-aged self-absorbed
    mother.

BILL
    John's middle-aged disinterested
    father.

CAMEO ROLES

MINETTE
    Also plays DENISE.

SHARON
    Also plays SUSAN and LADY.

BILL
    Also plays WRESTLING COACH.

ACT ONE SCENE ONE

A Cemetery. Future – Twenty Years.

*As the audience enters the theatre JOHN is sitting legs folded,
meditating. A beam of white light shines on him. John continues to
meditate as the audience takes their seats. Behind him are
gravestones with the names of the cast of characters except for
Nancy and John. Projected on wall is the current year plus twenty
years. It is twilight and turning into night as the audience takes
their seats. At curtain time NANCY enters.*

NANCY *(to audience)*
    Hello. Hi. Good evening everyone and
    welcome. My name is Nancy.   I hope this
    evening finds you well. This is John.
    Loves to meditate in this place. Finds his
    peace here. Me. I prefer something more
    'zen'. It is quiet here. I first met him
    about twenty years ago. Came to see me.
    I'm a doctor. Psychiatrist. After a few
    sessions I diagnosed him as what's the
    clinical term? Crazy as fuck. Sorry that
    was mean. A nice guy. A little slow. I
    will let you decide. I first tried to fix
    him with pills. But he wouldn't have
    anything to do with them.

Walks over to JOHN and picks up his diary.

NANCY
    His inner most thoughts. Page one. "I was
    born happy as a baby and screaming at the
    top of my lungs. And then I shit all over
    myself." You did see the notice about
    mature subject matter? Continuing. "It
    seems when we are born, we are connected to
    happiness and love. Then life happens.
    From then on you spend the rest of your
    life fighting back to that place. The
    Buddha called that place enlightenment or
    more practically simply happy. Content.
    At peace." You all are happy right?
    Right? I thought so. In this cemetery are
    all the people John has ever loved. A
    brief introduction if you will. Page
    sixteen. The parents. Sharon and Bill.

Spotlight on Sharon and Bill's gravestone.

NANCY
    Sharon and Bill Smith. *(reading from diary)*
    Sharon was silent this morning. Didn't say
    a word to Bill.

SHARON and BILL rise from behind their gravestones.

SHARON
    What did he say about me? Look at him. He
    looks so peaceful. I told you our son
    would turn out okay.

BILL
    Your son.

SHARON
  Our son. I always told him 'be a good
  boy'.

BILL
  For the record, my seed did not produce
  him.

Spotlight on ABAGAIL's gravestone. She rises.

ABAGAIL
  He is a good boy. Treated me with
  kindness.

SHARON
  And you are?

ABAGAIL
  Abagail. Mother Abagail.

SHARON
  Catholic?

ABAGAIL
  Sometimes.

NANCY
  The mother you choose.

SHARON
  What does that mean? I'm his mother. How
  many pages are dedicated to her?

NANCY
  Let's see. Quite a few.

SHARON
    When did he write me out of the story?

Spotlight on SEAN's gravestone. SEAN rises.

NANCY
    The boyfriend no one talked about.

SEAN
    Nice piece of ass.

SHARON
    You. You corrupted my son. I knew he
    would be in this.

SEAN *(cocky and proud)*
      I was in it alright.

BILL
    How ya doin Sean? Now that boy could play
    ball.

SHARON
    He's not what you think he is. What do you
    know? This happened after you died. You
    left me to deal with this.

ABAGAIL
    He loved him.

SHARON
    What do you know about love?

ABAGAIL
    I taught him about love.

SHARON
    I taught him before you. It's simple. Do
    as mommy says and I will love you. He's my
    son!

SEAN
    He called me daddy.

BILL
    Odd.

SHARON *(to SEAN)*
    Pervert. *(to BILL)* You have no clue.
    Never had.

HIM *(whispering from offstage)*
    He is mine! He is mine!

JOHN (AGE 55) *(to himself)*
    Mind be still.

Spotlight on gravestone directly behind JOHN. The name on the gravestone cannot be read. Ivy has grown over the stone.

SHARON
    What was that?

NANCY *(to audience)*
    This one. Harder to explain.

HIM rises. Hooded, faceless and all dressed in black. Grim Reaper style.

HIM
    He is mine. *(to ABAGAIL)* You are looking
    tired and haggard.

ABAGAIL
    Still tall, dark, and dark.

HIM
    You flatter me.

SHARON
    What is that?

*HIM stares down SEAN. SEAN cowers slightly. HIM walks over
to SHARON.*

HIM
    Bitch.

SHARON
    You're not a nice man.

NANCY *(to audience)*
    Buddha called him Mara.

JOHN (AGE 55)
    It is him.

NANCY
    The inner demon.

BILL
    Crazy as fuck!

SHARON, BILL, SEAN and ABAGAIL slowly exit. HIM approaches JOHN who opens his eyes from his meditation.

NANCY
    Twenty years ago. Late October I believe.

Projected Date moves backwards twenty years.

NANCY
    On the night before I first met John. Page
    forty-two. *(reading)* I found an old letter
    I wrote to my childhood hero. The
    televangelist reverend Oral Roberts. Dear
    Reverend Roberts.

NANCY exits.

ACT ONE SCENE TWO

DREAM. JOHN'S BEDROOM. NOW.

A thunderstorm rumbles.

JOHN (AGE 35)
Thank you so much for writing me back. I can't believe that you actually signed my letter. I hope the five dollars I sent helped out. Thank you for the cross. I will wear it always. Oh. I forgot to tell you that I am a Methodist too. I have been going to church ever since I can remember. I sing in the choir. Not very well. The choir director told me that Jesus said that it was okay if I just mouth the words. I pray for you and your ministry. I hope to grow up to be just like you. Your prayer partner. John. "Our father who art in heaven, hallow be thy name. Thy kingdom come, thy will be done on earth as it is in heaven. Give us today our daily bread. Forgive us our trespasses, as we forgive those who trespass against us. And lead us not into temptation. But deliver us from evil. For thyne is the kingdom, the power and the glory forever. Amen."

HIM steps forward from the shadows.

HIM
    Amen. Baby Jesus. Please forgive me.

JOHN *stiffens up.*

JOHN(AGE 35) *(stuttering)*
    You are not real.

HIM
    Who in the hell are you talking to now?

HIM reaches out to touch JOHN. JOHN reacts to his touch.

JOHN(AGE 35)
    I need my pills.

HIM
    There aren't any. You know I know your
    nasty little secrets.

JOHN(AGE 35)
    They are here somewhere.

HIM
    Shhh. Can you still hear the screaming?

JOHN(AGE 35)
    I don't remember any of it.

HIM
    I was there. You were there. Look at me.

JOHN (AGE 35)
    You have no face.

HIM
    You want to remove my mask? Go on John.
    It's really easy. Oh! It's all quiet now.
    You know what that means.

JOHN (AGE 35)
    No.

HIM
    The screaming has stopped. All good now.
    You know what tomorrow is? Training day.
    (singing) Stay in bed or you might be
    dead.

JOHN (AGE 35)   *(singing)*
    'Cause the horseman may come for your head.

HIM
    Well. Looky there. The little ground hog
    just caught a glimpse of his shadow. We
    had so much fun. Call me coach again.

JOHN (AGE 35)
    I'm confused.

HIM
    I know. Let's pray together. We are a
    team.

JOHN (AGE 35)
    "And there came a voice unto me, saying:
    Enos thy sins are forgiven thee, and thou
    shalt be blessed."

HIM *(mockingly)*
    "And I, Enos, knew that God 'could not lie;
    wherefore, my guilt was swept away."

JOHN (AGE 35)
    You are mocking me.

HIM
    Stop this religious bullshit. Only I care
    about you. The seed I planted will bear
    fruit. Continue my legacy. Hunting season
    is around the corner.

JOHN (AGE 35)
    You only exist in my mind.

HIM grabs JOHN by the throat.

HIM
    You try my patience boy. Acknowledge me.
    Love me!

JOHN (AGE 35)
    I have no secrets.

HIM
    Oh. You do. You really do. Here's a new
    one. *(whispering loudly in JOHN's ear)*
    What you resist persists. Remember me.

*HIM throws JOHN down. JOHN grasps for air. JOHN stumbles
to the couch. NANCY enters.*

ACT ONE SCENE THREE

NANCY'S OFFICE. NOW.

NANCY
How often do you have these dreams?

JOHN (AGE 35)
Nightly. For many years now. Should I call you doctor?

NANCY
Why not? I've busted my ass for years for the privilege. Really, I don't care.

JOHN (AGE 35)
Quite impressive certificates on your wall.

NANCY
That one is for Best Apple Pie at the Oklahoma State Fair.

JOHN (AGE 35)
I love the fair. Apple is my favorite.

NANCY
Banana Cream is mine.

JOHN (AGE 35)
My second favorite pie is Key Lime. Banana Cream is good too.

NANCY
    We agree. So, what can I do for you?

JOHN(AGE 35)
    You have my file. It's in there. You're
    number four. They passed me to you.

NANCY
    I think they just were trying to find
    someone that can better help you.

JOHN(AGE 35)
    The last doctor found God and the bottle.
    And Xanax.

NANCY
    Interesting.

JOHN(AGE 35)
    Do you believe in God?

NANCY
    Do we need an exorcist? Yes. I do. Just
    trying to be funny.

JOHN(AGE 35) *(Smiles)*
    I do like to laugh.

JOHN stares at the floor.

JOHN
    I'm scared.

NANCY *(emphasizing her accent)*
    It will be okay John. I know I sound like
    an Okie but I'm Harvard trained. I can
    help you. I'm not afraid.

JOHN (AGE 35)
    Like the others. You will be.

ACT ONE SCENE FOUR

JOHN'S CHILDHOOM HOME. PAST.

BILL and SHARON in the kitchen.

SHARON
   Bubba. Dinner's ready.

BILL
   What's he up to? He spends too much time
   in that room.

SHARON
   Got another letter from Oral Roberts.

BILL *(exasperated)*
   Jesus.

SHARON
   No. Oral. Bubba get in here.

JOHN(AGE 14) *(offstage)*
   Stop calling me that. My name is John.
   John.

BILL
   The boy realizes that the preacher does not
   personally write back.

SHARON
No he doesn't. Let it be and try acting
interested.

BILL
What do you mean by that?

JOHN enters for dinner.

JOHN(AGE 14)
Hi dad.

SHARON
Are you going to tell your father what you
got in the mail today?

JOHN(AGE 14)
I got a letter from Reverend Roberts today.
He signed it and all. I'm now one of his
prayer partners.

BILL
How much did that cost?

JOHN(AGE 14)
I sent him five dollars.

SHARON
He has been helping me out with chores
around the house.

JOHN(AGE 14)
He sent me this cross. It says 'partner'
on the back. I like it.

BILL has become interested in the news on TV.

```
JOHN(AGE 14)
   Maybe sometime we could drive to Tulsa to
   see him?

SHARON
   Maybe someday.
```

ACT ONE SCENE FIVE

NANCY'S OFFICE. NOW.

JOHN (AGE 35)
    I don't recall making the trip. After that
    I don't remember anything else.

NANCY
    That's fine. Just tell me what you can.
    Junior high? High school?

JOHN (AGE 35)
    My earliest memory of him was in high
    school. I was embarrassed.

NANCY
    It's an awkward time. Who is him?

ACT ONE SCENE SIX

A PARK. PAST.

JOHN's first date with MINETTE in high school. MINETTE carries a motorcycle black jacket and puts it on JOHN.

JOHN (AGE 35)
    Him. I wasn't sure if he was there for me
    or Minette.

NANCY
    You're girlfriend?

JOHN (AGE 35)
    My first time. Attempt. Like my jacket?
    I bought this for my first date.

MINETTE
    I like your jacket.

JOHN (AGE 17) *(to MINETTE)*
    Thanks.

JOHN (AGE 35) *(to NANCY)*
    My dad liked it too. I looked sexy and
    tough in it. She liked me, my jacket and
    my Broadway show tunes.

NANCY moves back out of the scene.

MINETTE
    This is such a beautiful place at night.
    The blue lights of the runway are so
    pretty.

JOHN (AGE 17)
    I like coming here. I always wonder where
    the planes are headed. I can sit here for
    hours watching each plane till I can't see
    it anymore. See that plane. I bet it's
    headed to Dallas.

MINETTE
    You did a great job today.

JOHN (AGE 17)
    The play wasn't that good. I mispronounced
    that work again.
    (stuttering the word abominable)
    Abominable. Abominable. I still can't
    fricken' say that word. They laughed at
    me.

MINETTE
    I didn't. It's okay to say fucking if your
    mad.

JOHN (AGE 17)
    Our teacher hates me. I know she thinks I
    am the worst actor in the school.

MINETTE
    Then why did she give you a lead. Come
    here. I want to show you something.

JOHN (AGE 17)
    Oh.

MINETTE gives him a peak at her breasts. They kiss.

MINETTE
    I'm ready.

JOHN (AGE 17)
    Are you sure?

MINETTE kisses JOHN. In the shadows HIM appears.

JOHN
    Did you see that?

MINETTE
    See what?

JOHN (AGE 17)
    Look over there.

MINETTE
    Where?

JOHN (AGE 17)
    By the tree.

MINETTE
    It's the airport police.

JOHN (AGE 17)
    Maybe we should go.

MINETTE
    Why? We're not doing anything wrong. He's
    probably likes to watch. I hardly think we
    are the first to be parked here.

JOHN (AGE 17)
    It's just weird.

MINETTE
    You're always so paranoid.

JOHN (AGE 17)
    Since when?

MINETTE
    Remember when you got pulled over for
    speeding on First Street. You acted like
    you were going to jail.

JOHN (AGE 17)
    I couldn't afford a ticket.

MINETTE
    Uh uh! Look he's leaving. Obviously,
    we're boring him. Perhaps I should show
    him my tits.

HIM steps back but is not completely gone.

JOHN (AGE 17)
    Stop it.

MINETTE
    I like men in uniforms.

JOHN (AGE 17)
    I have a uniform. You never ask me to wear
    it.

MINETTE
> Cub scouts? Not what I had in mind. It
> still fits don't it?

JOHN (AGE 17)
> Ouch!

MINETTE
> You know I love you.

MINETTE grabs him, and they kiss again. More clothes get removed.

JOHN (AGE 17)
> Sorry. Sorry. I need to pee before we
> start.

MINETTE
> I will be waiting.

JOHN exits the car. It is cold outside. He stares in the direction of where HIM was standing. HIM moves forward. JOHN returns to the car and climbs on top of MINETTE.

MINETTE
> Your hands are cold and you're shaking.

JOHN (AGE 17)
> It's cold out there.

JOHN is still looking at HIM.

MINETTE
    Forget the cop. Hello. I'm here.

They kiss again. JOHN tries but fails.

JOHN(AGE 17)
    It's not working. It got too cold.

MINETTE
    Let's try something else.

MINETTE goes down on him. MINETTE exits and takes JOHN's leather jacket with her.

ACT ONE SCENE SEVEN

A HIGH SCHOOL GYM. PAST.

JOHN (AGE 35) *(To NANCY)*
    A blow job didn't work either. I couldn't
    get the man in the shadows out of my mind.
    It was very confusing to me. Either way,
    it felt like a huge failure. A rite of
    passage that just passed. It had to be a
    lack of testosterone. I could fix this. I
    decided to play sports

WRESTLING COACH and SEAN enters ready to wrestle.

NANCY
    And who is he?

WRESTLING COACH hands JOHN his head gear.

JOHN (AGE 35)
    Sean Cunningham. State wrestling champ two
    years in a row.

WRESTLING COACH
    Okay Smith your up next. You and
    Cunningham.

The coach blows his whistle. SEAN and JOHN begin to wrestle. SEAN pins JOHN quickly.

WRESTLING COACH
    Seven seconds. A personal best Cunningham.

JOHN (AGE 17) *(to COACH)*
    Give me another chance. One more time.

SEAN pins him again even faster. They stand face to face.

JOHN (AGE 17)
    Again!

SEAN pins JOHN. Stays on top of him. They stare at each other.

WRESTLING COACH
    Okay. Smith you had enough now? Break up.
    Let's move.

SEAN and JOHN are slow to move.

WRESTLING COACH
    Hit the showers. Pizza night.

JOHN (AGE 35) *(to NANCY referencing his hard
on)*
    It worked that time. I hope he didn't
    notice.

SEAN leaves with WRESTLING COACH then returns.

SEAN
   Hey.

JOHN (AGE 17)
   You're pretty good.

SEAN
   I didn't mean to embarrass you. Coach can
   be an ass.

JOHN (AGE 17)
   This isn't for me.

SEAN
   You seemed to enjoy it.

JOHN (AGE 17)
   Your friends are waiting for you.

SEAN
   I don't feel like pizza tonight. You like
   Chinese?

JOHN (AGE 17)
   Sure.

SEAN
   Meet you outside. After they leave.

JOHN (AGE 17)
   Okay.

SEAN exits.

JOHN(AGE 35)
   I enjoy looking at him. Still do. After
   all these years. Mom even in her grave
   still has issues with our special
   friendship.

NANCY
   Sean Cunningham. Is this the same Sean?
   NFL Sean? Superbowl Sean?

JOHN(AGE 35)
   This stays in this room. We are together
   but separate. Very, very close friends.
   It is for his benefit and mine. He hides
   me from the world in plain sight. He has
   always protected me. Made the bullies go
   away. He once decked a guy for making fun
   of me. I stutter at times. That cost him
   a lot of money. The media thought he was
   being chivalrous with about a woman. I
   don't know why he keeps me around.

NANCY
   Maybe he loves you. Tell me more about
   what is going on now in your life.

ACT ONE SCENE EIGHT

SEAN AND JOHN'S HOME. NOW.

SEAN
  You're up early.

JOHN (AGE 35)
  I've got a project to get done. Due by
  ten.

SEAN
  I'm due in at nine at the training center.
  Then a game tonight.

JOHN (AGE 35)
  Who are you playing?

SEAN
  Schedule is on the fridge. You can sit in
  the suite.

JOHN (AGE 35)
  No thanks. Then I'd have to talk to your
  trophy wife. Sorry.

SEAN
  I take care of you. Did you take the
  recycling out?

JOHN (AGE 35)
  No. Not yet.

SEAN
It's nearly seven-thirty. The truck has
probably already been here. Where's your
head lately?

JOHN (AGE 35)
My heads just fine. I'll do it.

SEAN
Never mind. I'll take care of it. Did you
call your sister?

JOHN (AGE 35)
What is this? I'll call her.

SEAN
Your nephew's graduation is in three weeks.
I don't suppose you have looked at airline
flights either.

JOHN (AGE 35)
Sean please. I got to get this done. Not
now.

SEAN
It just seems I have to do everything
around here.

JOHN (AGE 35)
She gets a maid. I've got to work.

SEAN
This is my home. Where you going?

JOHN (AGE 35)
Bathroom.

JOHN goes into the bathroom.

SEAN
    We are still going to have this
    conversation. Maybe you can clean the
    bathroom while you are in there.

JOHN(AGE 35)
    I wouldn't have to if you didn't get shit
    all over the toilet seat. ESPN Headline.
    Superbowl Sean and his Superbowl shits.

SEAN
    Well at least my ass can produce some
    excitement. Unlike yours lately.

JOHN(AGE 35) *(stuttering)*
    Go fuck yourself!

*HIM enters and is looking at JOHN. JOHN is stressing and biting
his finger. JOHN looks over at him.*

HIM
    Still biting the finger?

JOHN(AGE 35)
    Yes.

HIM
    I can help you stop it.

JOHN(AGE 35)
    I can control it on my own.

HIM
    Here let me help you.

HIM directs him to a razor blade.

SEAN
    John!

JOHN (AGE 35)
    Just a minute!

HIM guides his hand to pick up the razor blade. They both cut his finger. JOHN bleeds.

HIM
    Beautiful isn't it. Go on. Go on.

JOHN tastes the blood.

HIM
    Peace. Peace.

SEAN
    I don't want to fight but we do need to
    discuss this. John. John. Are you
    listening to me? I'm not going away until
    we discuss this. This is just like you. I
    am trying to have a meaningful conversation
    and you have to pee. You pee more than
    anyone I know.

JOHN is relaxed and puts the razor blade away. HIM exits.

JOHN (AGE 35)
    Sean I'm sorry. I have been a little
    stressed lately and I know you are
    frustrated with me. I'm sorry. You are
    right. I will do better. You have every
    right to be angry with me.

SEAN
    I don't mean to nag.

JOHN cleans up and exits the bathroom.

JOHN (AGE 35)
    I know. I'm sorry.

JOHN lovingly hugs SEAN.

JOHN
    I love you.

SEAN
    I love you too.

JOHN (AGE 35)
    I will make the reservations. Party of two
    or three?

SEAN
    Just me and you. Not her.

JOHN(AGE 35)
    Good answer.

SEAN
    Is my shit that bad?

JOHN(AGE 35)
    Let's just leave it at a hug. Don't get
    hurt tonight.

SEAN
    Have a good day. Love ya. Don't forget to
    feed the dog.

ACT ONE SCENE NINE

NANCY'S OFFICE. NOW.

NANCY
  When did this happen?

JOHN (AGE 35)
  Last week. Sean doesn't know. He knows
  about my nightmares, but this is old news.
  He has to wake me up often.

NANCY
  How long have you been cutting yourself?

JOHN (AGE 35)
  Years. Ever since high school. That
  evening after my date with Minette I went
  to the backyard and smoked a joint. He
  followed me home.

NANCY
  The cop?

JOHN (AGE 35)
  Him. He's not a cop. I heard his heavy
  footsteps walking behind my house as I got
  high. I sat there quietly. Did he know I
  was there? I took a knife I found and cut
  myself while I masturbated. I felt he was
  watching me. After I came. His footsteps
  faded into the night. I knew he was…

pleased with me. I laid there silently
until my cum dried looking up at the stars.

NANCY
    Perhaps it was the pot. Are you sure he or
    him was really behind the fence?

JOHN (AGE 35)
    No. I've never questioned it. What do you
    think?

NANCY
    Based on what I know thus far. You show
    signs of PTSD. Post-traumatic stress
    disorder.

JOHN (AGE 35)
    I see. I've been missing my mother this
    week.

NANCY
    Is she still alive?

JOHN (AGE 35)
    No. She passed away about 10 years ago.
    She lived about 15 years past my dad.

NANCY
    How would you describe her?

JOHN (AGE 35)
    She was very protective. She was always
    trying to make up for my fathers' lack of
    attention. It was very smothering. I
    don't mean to take anything away from her.
    She gave me anything I ever wanted.

NANCY
    Surely not everything. What mother does?

JOHN (AGE 35)
    Yeah. I guess. She did take my minibike
    away from me.

NANCY
    To go along with your black jacket?

JOHN (AGE 35)
    This was way before that. I was fourteen
    years old. There was this local toy store
    called 'Kiddie City'. I registered in a
    drawing and won the grand prize which was
    this Minibike called a 'Wild Cat'. I loved
    that bike. It was kinda frustrating
    because my mother would only let me ride it
    in the front yard. Hard to be a 'bad ass'
    in a front yard. But I tried my best.
    Anyway, after a couple of weeks she thought
    it was a good idea to get rid of it. I was
    so upset. You know my father did nothing.
    This is where 'dad' is supposed to step in
    and let a boy be a boy. But he didn't. So
    we sold it.

NANCY
    That must have angered you.

JOHN (AGE 35)
    I guess.

NANCY
    Did you tell her?

JOHN (AGE 35)
    No. As usual I just smiled and agreed and
    said she was right. But inside I was
    upset. So, I went for a walk.

NANCY
    Where did you go?

JOHN (AGE 35)
    To the store. We had this corner market in
    the neighborhood. I would go there and get
    an icy.

NANCY
    Was that common?

JOHN (AGE 35)
    Sure. All us neighborhood kids would go up
    there or walk even further down to the T,G
    & Y. It was like a Target. Along the way
    I was so mad I couldn't even cry about it.

ACT ONE SCENE TEN

THE CORNER MARKET. NOW.

JOHN approaches the store. SAM, a security officer greets him. He rides a motorcycle.

SAM
    You look sad.

JOHN(AGE 14)
    A little.

SAM
    Are you okay?

JOHN(AGE 14)
    I'm fine.

SAM
    Live near here?

JOHN(AGE 14)
    A few blocks that way. I like your bike.
    I used to have one. Not this big.

SAM
    You did. What kind of bike?

JOHN(AGE 14)
    A Wild Cat.

SAM
    Sounds impressive.

JOHN (AGE 14)
    Mom made me sell it.

SAM
    I knew you were sad.

JOHN (AGE 14)
    Why do parents do things like that?

SAM
    I wouldn't do that to my son.

JOHN (AGE 14)
    How old is your son?

SAM
    I don't have kids.

JOHN (AGE 14)
    You get lonely?

SAM
    Why you ask that?

JOHN (AGE 14)
    You look lonely.

SAM
    I do? And you?

JOHN (AGE 14)
    Sometimes.

SAM
    I'm Sam.

JOHN (AGE 14)
    John.

SAM
    Nice to meet you.

JOHN (AGE 14) *(stuttering)*
    Nice to meet. Same here. Sorry.

SAM
    Don't apologize. The way you talk is cute.
    Special.

SAM puts JOHN on the motorcycle.

JOHN (AGE 14)
    What is this?

SAM
    It's a Harley.

JOHN (AGE 14)
    Wow.

SAM
    Good to see you smile boy. Want something
    to drink? Hungry?

JOHN (AGE 14)
    Sure.

SAM
    Do you like chocolate?

JOHN(AGE 14)
    Mom would be mad about the candy this close
    to dinner.

SAM
    It can be our secret. You listen to me.

JOHN(AGE 14)
    Okay.

SAM
    Eat your chocolate. I'll give you a ride
    home.

JOHN(AGE 14)
    Thanks.

HIM enters. JOHN stares at HIM. NANCY enters. SAM exits.

NANCY
    What is it John? John?

JOHN(AGE 35)
    I need to walk. I'm done.

ACT ONE SCENE ELEVEN

THE PARK. NOW. LATER THAT NIGHT.

*Late night. ABAGAIL lies on a bench sleeping. JOHN looks at her.
HIM is standing next to JOHN.*

```
HIM
    I remember my first one.

JOHN (AGE 35)
    Let me think.

HIM
    It's time.

JOHN (AGE 35)
    Not tonight.

HIM
    We went shopping together.
```

HIM guides knife out of JOHN's pocket.

```
JOHN (AGE 35)
    I'm not ready.
```

HIM
    Just like riding a bike.

JOHN (AGE 35)
    What's that supposed to mean?

HIM
    I told you to pay cash for that.

JOHN (AGE 35)
    I can't do this.

HIM
    She's perfect. She's sleeping. She won't
    be missed. She's passed out. No struggle.
    It's the perfect starter kit.

JOHN (AGE 35)
    You're not funny.

HIM
    Come here.

HIM lovingly places JOHN against his chest.

HIM
    Remember the promise you made me.

JOHN snuggles into HIM's chest.

HIM
    It's okay. Do me proud.

JOHN takes the knife and approaches the woman.

```
HIM
   Do it.
```

JOHN raises the knife. The woman stirs.

```
JOHN(AGE 35)
   She moved!

HIM
   Play it cool.
```

ABAGAIL rises from sleep. HIM fades back.

```
ABAGAIL
   Looks like you just seen a ghost.

JOHN(AGE 35)
   I'm sorry.

ABAGAIL
   Sorry about what child?

JOHN(AGE 35)
   Nothing.  Sorry I didn't hear what you
   said.

ABAGAIL
   Listen.  Hear that?

JOHN(AGE 35)
   What?
```

ABAGAIL
    Listen.

JOHN(AGE 35)
    I don't hear anything.

ABAGAIL
    Precisely. The sound of nothing. Care to
    join me?

JOHN(AGE 35)
    I've got to get going.

ABAGAIL pulls out an apple.

ABAGAIL
    I understand. Got a knife?

JOHN(AGE 35)
    Yes.

JOHN hands knife to her. She peels apple.

ABAGAIL
    Quite the blade. In the Bible apples got a
    bad rap. Shame. They have always been so
    tasty.

ABAGAIL offers a slice. JOHN accepts.

JOHN(AGE 35)
    They are good.

ABAGAIL's purse falls to ground spilling contents. JOHN picks up her items.

ABAGAIL
   Very nice.

JOHN (AGE 35)
   Do you need money?

ABAGAIL
   No dear. I have plenty. 'Bout time
   another one falls from the tree.

Apple falls from tree.

ABAGAIL
   It's yours.

JOHN (AGE 35) *(Confused and amazed)*
   Thanks. I do need to go.

ABAGAIL
   See you again?

JOHN (AGE 35)
   Sure.

ABAGAIL
   Trust her. She will help you.

JOHN (AGE 35)
   Her?

ABAGAIL
   The woman you call Nancy.

JOHN(AGE 35)
   Nancy? Who are you?

ABAGAIL
   Someone who loves you.

JOHN(AGE 35)
   I don't know you.

ABAGAIL
   Of course, you do. We just met. I'm
   Abagail.

JOHN(AGE 35)
   John.

ABAGAIL
   I know you have questions. I don't mean to
   add to the storm in your mind. You know
   darkness. I'm here to remind you of the
   light. The heart. Look into my eyes and
   know that I am good.

JOHN(AGE 35)
   Are you an angel? This can't be.

ABAGAIL
   You believe in Him. Why can't you believe
   in me?

JOHN(AGE 35)
   Am I being punished?

ABAGAIL
   No dear. Forgiveness was immediate. You
   have dug yourself into a deep hole. I'm
   your lifeline. Only you can pull yourself
   up.

JOHN (AGE 35)
    How?

ABAGAIL
    I just opened a memory in you. You are
    going to have to drag that demon into the
    light. Kicking and screaming.

JOHN (AGE 35)
    I feel powerless.

ABAGAIL
    The women in red will give you the kick in
    the ass you need. Pack a flashlight and
    shine a light on it. That's all you need
    to do.

JOHN (AGE 35)
    Can I get you a room?

ABAGAIL
    Not necessary. Very kind of you. Good to
    see your heart coming alive again.

JOHN (AGE 35)
    I hope to see you again.

ABACAIL
    If it is meant to be.

JOHN (AGE 35)
    Goodnight.

*HIM reminds JOHN of his presence. JOHN exits. HIM and
ABAGAIL acknowledge each other.*

HIM
    A bag lady? He doesn't have it in him.

ABAGAIL
    We'll see. Let the games begin.

HIM
    Time for a quickie?

ABAGAIL
    Why not? Be nice. If you call me bitch
    again, I will cut your dick off with that
    knife.

ABAGAIL bends over.

ACT ONE SCENE TWELVE

THE CORNER MARKET. PAST.

NANCY enters wearing red. SAM enters.

JOHN(AGE 35) *(to NANCY)*
    Yes. I remember going back a few times and
    Sam was often around. He seemed to care
    about me. Always bought me things.
    Whatever I wanted. Candy and sodas.

SAM is smoking. Hands JOHN some candy.

SAM
    Your favorite.

JOHN(AGE 14)
    Thanks. I love these.

SAM
    Watch this.

SAM blows smoke rings.

JOHN (AGE 35) *(to NANCY)*
    Then he made a big smoke ring which floated
    forever. He would look at me and not say a
    word. Mainly I guess because I kept
    talking. He never told me to stop talking.
    He just listened. No one had ever listened
    to me before. At least without
    complaining. I hadn't noticed that I had
    stopped stuttering.

SAM
    How was school today?

JOHN (AGE 14)
    Fine. I'm doing a play.

SAM
    A play? What's is it about?

JOHN (AGE 14)
    The headless horseman of Sleepy Hollow.

SAM
    Don't know.

JOHN
    Can I tell you?

SAM
    Sure kid.

JOHN
    It's about a schoolteacher named Ichabod
    Crane who moves to Sleepy Hollow. However,
    the place is haunted.

LADY, a long blonde-haired woman, walks by and catches the eye of SAM. He cruises her very intently admiring her.

JOHN
    At night there is rider with no head.

SAM
    Damn.

JOHN(AGE 14)
    He roams around at night looking to chop
    someone's head off.

SAM
    Really? A head. Shouldn't you be doing
    something like Winnie the Pooh. You're too
    sweet for stuff like that.

JOHN(AGE 14)
    I wrote a song. *(singing)* A horseman rides
    in the middle of the night. Pull your
    covers up 'cause it's a fright. Stay in
    bed or you might be dead.

SAM *(to LADY)*
    Hello.

JOHN(AGE 14) *(continues singing)*
    0'Cause the horseman may come for your
    head.

LADY
    Hello.

SAM
    Sam.

LADY *(to JOHN)*
   And you are?

SAM
   John. This is my boy John.

LADY
   Your son?

SAM
   Foster son. Police Athletic League.

LADY
   How sweet. You are lucky to have such a
   nice police officer looking over you. *(to
   SAM)* Married. Sorry.

SAM
   Have a good day 'mam.

JOHN(AGE 14) *(continues singing)*
   A horseman rides in the middle of the
   night. Pull your covers up cause it's a
   fright. Stay in bed or you might be dead.
   Cause the horseman may come for your head.

They both laugh.

SAM
   I need you to pay attention when a lady is
   around. Show respect.

JOHN(AGE 14)
   Yeah.

SAM
  Men like the attention of a pretty woman.

JOHN (AGE 14)
  My friends and I try to stay away from
  them.

SAM
  That will change. When a lady approaches,
  I need you to be cute. Use what you got.

JOHN (AGE 14)
  Another secret?

SAM
  Yeah.

SAM puts his arm around JOHN.

JOHN (AGE 35) *(to NANCY)*
  He took me under his wing. The father I
  never had.

NANCY
  Not exactly the best lesson.

JOHN (AGE 35) *(unusual expression of anger)*
  He liked me!

NANCY
  Tell me more about your father.

SAM fades to background. BILL enters.

JOHN (AGE 35)
   What do you want to know?

NANCY
   Did he spend much time with you?

JOHN (AGE 35)
   No. Not really.

NANCY
   You mentioned before you were quite the
   actor. Did he go to your plays?

JOHN (AGE 35)
   He was always working during school hours.
   No. He never attended.

NANCY
   Do you have any good memories about him?

JOHN (AGE 35)
   One time he invited me to go on a trip to
   San Antonio with him. It was just him and
   me.

NANCY
   How old were you?

JOHN (AGE 35)
   Fourteen. He took me to all of my favorite
   places. There was this small amusement
   park it had a small ferris wheel and a
   roller coaster. Then the best part he took
   me to the Tower of the Americas to eat. It
   was beautiful. You could see all over the
   city. I had fried chicken.

JOHN and BILL are at dinner.

BILL
    Are you having a good time?

JOHN(AGE 14)
    Yes. Thanks for bringing me here.

BILL
    I want you to have fun. Just me and you.

JOHN(AGE 14)
    I am.

BILL
    Your kind of quiet tonight.

JOHN(AGE 14)
    I'm fine. I know you don't like it when I
    talk too much.

BILL
    You just sometimes ramble on about things
    that no one cares. Things that others can't
    relate to. I'm just trying to teach you to
    be interesting. Trust me you will thank me
    when you are older.

JOHN(AGE 14)
    I understand.

BILL
    Tell me something interesting.

JOHN(AGE 14)
    My friend Mike and I are working on a play
    at school.

BILL
   A play?

JOHN (AGE 14)
   Yes. Sleepy Hollow.

BILL
   You really should get out and play some
   sports with the guys.

JOHN (AGE 14)
   I've tried. I'm just not good at that.

BILL
   Perhaps you should try harder. There is
   bound to be a sport you can do.

JOHN (AGE 14)
   I'm am good at.

BILL
   Ice skating isn't a sport for guys.

JOHN (AGE 14)
   Dad?

BILL
   Yes.

JOHN (AGE 14)
   Why?

BILL
   Why what?

JOHN (AGE 14)
   I look at my friend Mark. He and his
   father. Well it's different.

BILL
    Different? What do you mean?

JOHN (AGE 14)
    They do things differently together.

BILL
    Spit it out. What are you talking about?

SAM moves forward. JOHN leaves his father and walks over to SAM.

SAM
    Sorry I missed your play kid. How was it?
    Did he get his head?

JOHN (AGE 14)
    No. Ichabod got away in the end.

SAM
    Sometimes that happens.

JOHN (AGE 14)
    I like to think so.

SAM
    Was your dad there?

JOHN (AGE 14)
    No. He had to work.

SAM
    Really. You got a sorry dad boy. This
    shit pisses me off.

JOHN (AGE 14)
    It's okay. It was just a stupid play.

SAM
    He hurt you, didn't he?

JOHN (AGE 14)
    No.

SAM
    Don't lie to me.

JOHN (AGE 14)
    No.

SAM
    I care about you.

SAM exits.

BILL
    John. What are you talking about?

JOHN walks back over to his father.

JOHN (AGE 14)
    I just need to know something. Do you love
    me?

BILL
    Who has put these crazy thoughts in your
    head?

JOHN (AGE 35) *(to NANCY)*
  Stop!

NANCY
  Keep going John.

SAM *(offstage voice over)*
  He ain't no good.

JOHN (AGE 35) *(to NANCY stammering hard)*
  I'm confused.

Flashes of light. HIM enters.

JOHN (AGE 35)
  He's here. I see him.

NANCY
  Who do you see?

JOHN (AGE 35)
  Him. He's in my head. He's always been in
  there.

NANCY
  Who is him? He hasn't always been there.
  The only way we can get to the bottom of
  this is for you to face it.

HIM walks over to JOHN.

JOHN (AGE 35)
  He's talking to me.

HIM
    I would love to see those pretty eyes again
    without this mask.

JOHN (AGE 35)
    Get away from me.

SAM *(offstage voice over)*
    Your father is shit.

NANCY
    Who?

JOHN (AGE 35)
    Him. He's here.

NANCY
    Who? Your father? Who is it?

HIM
    You really don't need her. Remember.

JOHN (AGE 35)
    I don't remember.

HIM
    Where's my boy?

JOHN (AGE 35)
    Stay away from him.

NANCY
    What's he saying?

JOHN (AGE 35)
    Can't you see him?

NANCY *(playing along)*
    Yes. I can see him. But only you can
    understand what he is saying.

JOHN (AGE 35)
    He wants to talk to the boy. I won't let
    him.

SAM *(offstage voice over)*
    I would have been there for you.

NANCY
    John stop protecting him. Allow him to
    talk.

HIM
    Come boy.

JOHN turns away from HIM.

JOHN (AGE 35)
    Stay back.

HIM
    You made your choice.

JOHN (AGE 35)
    What choice?

HIM
    You don't recall. Daddy didn't give you an
    answer.

JOHN (AGE 35)
    I'm not going to ask him again.

NANCY
   Ask him John.

JOHN(AGE 14) *(to BILL)*
Dad.

BILL approaches and stands next to JOHN.

BILL
   What is it?

JOHN(AGE 14)
   Do you love me?

JOHN(AGE 35)
   He's not answering us.

SAM *(offstage voice over)*
   I told you.

HIM
   I told you.

JOHN(AGE 35) *(Yelling)*
   Why don't you answer him? You son of a
   bitch! Answer him!

*BILL reaches over and just pats him on the head. HIM extends his
hand to JOHN.*

JOHN *(to NANCY)*
   Answer him. He didn't answer me. He just
   sat there looking at me and asked me what I
   wanted for dessert.

NANCY
   I'm sorry. I'm so sorry.

HIM and SAM *(offstage voice over)*
   You will be.

JOHN walks over to HIM. HIM gets down to his level. JOHN touches his face with curiosity and removes the hood to reveal his face. It is SAM. SAM smiles and touches his face.

SAM
   Come ride with me.

JOHN (AGE 35) *(to NANCY)*
   Please don't go. He's going with him.

JOHN (AGE 14)
   Can we go fast?

SAM
   My horse knows no other speed. Look at me.
   Mind your mouth. Keep the secret.

JOHN (AGE 35)
   I will.

SAM
   Ready?

JOHN and SAM walk off hand in hand.

JOHN (AGE 35) *(to NANCY)*
   They're leaving together.

NANCY
    Let them go.

NANCY
    Let them go.

ACT TWO SCENE ONE

THE CORNER MARKET. PAST.

SAM and JOHN are standing next to his motorcycle.

SAM
    Well?

JOHN(AGE 14)
    That was fast. And loud.

SAM
    Glad you liked it.

JOHN(AGE 14)
    I want one of these.

SAM
    Someday.

JOHN(AGE 14)
    When?

SAM
    Learn patience.

JOHN(AGE 14)
    What's that?

SAM
    It means waiting your turn. Can't get what
    you want. When you want.

JOHN (AGE 14)
    Are you patience?

SAM
    Patient. And no.

JOHN (AGE 14)
    How old are you?

SAM
    Old enough. Let's play a game.

JOHN (AGE 14)
    What kind of game?

SAM
    Shhh! Simon says.

JOHN (AGE 14)
    I'm good at Simon says.

SAM
    Really?

JOHN (AGE 14)
    Try me.

SAM
    Touch your nose.

JOHN doesn't touch his nose.

SAM
    Good. Simon says touch your nose.

JOHN touches his nose.

SAM
    Simon says give me a hug.

JOHN hugs SAM.

SAM
    You're doing good. Look at me.

JOHN looks at him. SAM slaps him in the face.

SAM
    Don't cry.

JOHN (AGE 14)
    I'm not.

SAM
    Simon says turn the other cheek.

JOHN offers the other cheek. SAM raises his hand and smiles.

SAM
    I had to see if you could take it.

JOHN (AGE 14) *(stuttering)*
    I can take it. I've been hit before.

SAM
    Who hit you?

JOHN (AGE 14)
    Greg.

SAM
    I'll fuck him up.

JOHN (AGE 14)
    It's okay. You would do that for me?

SAM
    I protect what's mine. Do you ever get
    pissed?

JOHN (AGE 14)
    I guess. No.

SAM
    Everyone is angry about something.

JOHN (AGE 14)
    Has anyone ever laughed at you?

SAM
    Not for long. What happened with him?

JOHN (AGE 14)
    Greg hit me because I wanted to be a
    cheerleader.

SAM busts out laughing.

SAM
    No. No. Not that. A cheerleader?

JOHN (AGE 14)
    We were playing a game of football. No one
    picked me. I was left on the sidelines to
    cheer. What else could I do?

SAM
    You could have been the water boy.

JOHN (AGE 14)
    There are guy cheerleaders.

SAM
    If you want to be a cheerleader. We'll
    make it happen.

JOHN (AGE 14)
    When did they laughed at you?

SAM pauses and then quietly.

SAM
    I stuttered too. Called me stupid.

JOHN (AGE 14)
    I'm sorry they hurt you.

SAM
    Me too. I guess you and I are two peas in
    a pod.

SAM rubs JOHN's head.

SAM
    I'm sorry you met me.

JOHN (AGE 14)
    Why?

SAM
    I'm sorry you met me.

JOHN (AGE 14)
    Why?

ACT TWO SCENE TWO

NANCY'S OFFICE. NOW.

JOHN(AGE 35)
   I'm tired.

NANCY
   You had a big breakthrough today. You've
   suppressed this a long time. It can be
   tiring. Don't push it. Now that the flood
   gate has been open. This will come as it
   comes.

JOHN(AGE 35)
   No worries. I do feel better. Not as
   crazy.

NANCY
   Tell me something good.

JOHN(AGE 35)
   My partner scored two touchdowns last
   night.

NANCY
   Did you go?

JOHN(AGE 35)
   Yes. Always when I can. I enjoy his
   games. He does this end zone dance. Makes
   this warrior face. I just smile 'cause I…

know what it means. Makes the same face
when he cums. Orgasms.

NANCY

Happy endings. Do others know about the
two of you?

JOHN(AGE 35)

Only you. And mom. I respect his privacy.
Those close to us see us as lifelong
friends. It's funny when I'm at work and
the guys are all talking about him the next
day. I just smile. Some secrets are fun.

NANCY

Does the secrecy of your relationship
bother you?

SHARON enters.

JOHN(AGE 35)

I think I would be lying if I said no. I'm
used to it.

SHARON

You never considered my feelings.

JOHN(AGE 35) *(to NANCY)*

There's some lingering guilt.

SHARON

How could I explain this to your
grandmother? Much less my friends.

JOHN(AGE 35)

It wasn't a choice. God forced this on me.

NANCY *(not hearing the internal dialogue in JOHN's mind)*
    John?

SHARON
    God had nothing to do with this. I took
    you to church. What happened?

JOHN (AGE 35)
    What happened?

SHARON
    I'll never forget the day I saw you and
    Sean. You said you were praying. Praying
    my ass.

JOHN (AGE 35)
    I didn't know what else to say.

SHARON
    Hard to speak with a mouth full.
    Sacrilegious.   I did not teach you that.

JOHN (AGE 35)
    No. You didn't.

SHARON
    You are my only son. I will always love
    you. But I cannot understand this. Live
    your life. But don't let me see it. Or
    any of my friends.

SHARON exits.

JOHN (AGE 35) *(to NANCY)*
    It still lingers.

NANCY
    Did your Mom ever meet Sam?

JOHN (AGE 35)
    She did. Loved him. So did my father. He
    slowly invaded my life. He had different
    looks. When I first met him, he looked
    like a cop. The next time he looked like a
    Hell's Angel. My parents knew him as a
    counselor at the local YMCA. Here to save
    me by teaching me manly things like sports.
    My father was thrilled. They never minded
    the time I spent with him.

SAM enters dressed as a coach with whistle.

NANCY
    He was popular?

JOHN (AGE 35)
    Definitely. However, looking back on him
    as an adult. He was lonely.

NANCY
    Most are. Even in a crowd.

SAM and JOHN are standing face to face.

JOHN (AGE 35)
    I was too. A match made in hell.

SAM
    It's training day. Walk with me.

JOHN (AGE 35)
    Yes.

SAM
    This ain't gonna be easy.

JOHN (AGE 35)
    I know.

SAM
    Ready?

JOHN (AGE 35)
    Yes.

SAM
    Yes, what?

JOHN (AGE 35)
    Yes, Sir!

SAM blows his whistle.

JOHN *(to NANCY)*
    He ran my ass off. We often took rides on
    his motorcycle. I remember my cheek
    pressed up against his leathered back.
    Hiding from the cold wind. One day he
    stopped on this old dirt road. He made me
    run behind his bike.

SAM
    Tough you up.

JOHN (AGE 35)
    He often told me. Push-ups. Jumping rope.
    You name it. Gave me my first taste of a
    beer. Didn't like it. Still don't. He
    liked beer. And women. Lots of them.
    Most nights we would end our training
    sessions with a treat at the corner market.
    He had a beer. Me. A slurpy.

ACT TWO SCENE THREE

THE CORNER MARKET. PAST.

JOHN(AGE 14)
   I got an A on my math test.

SAM
   Good for you. Here I got something for
   you?

JOHN(AGE 14)
   What?

SAM
   Open it. It's a surprise.

JOHN(AGE 14)
   A gift. It's not my birthday.

SAM
   Go on. Open it.

JOHN(AGE 14)
   I'm sorry I don't have a gift for you.

SAM
   Some other day.

JOHN(AGE 14)
   What is it?

The gift is a necklace.

SAM
   My father gave this to me.

JOHN (AGE 14)
   Wow.

SAM
   And now it is yours.

JOHN (AGE 14)
   Thanks.

SAM
   I want you to be my son.

JOHN (AGE 14)
   But my dad.

SAM *(Coldly)*
   If you need to run back to him. I
   understand.

JOHN (AGE 14)
   No. He doesn't want me.

SAM
   Then it's settled. Between me and you.
   This is a secret you know.

JOHN (AGE 14) *(confused)*
   Sure. I can keep a secret.

SAM puts the necklace on JOHN

SAM

Now, I need a wife. You can help me find
her.

JOHN (AGE 35) *(to NANCY)*

A wing man in training. He coached me on
acting cute. Coached me on what to say. I
was surprisingly good at it. All he would
say was.

SAM

Find me a wife.

JOHN (AGE 35)

And off I went. I would get them together.
The girl left with him. I would go home.
After a while we started hanging out at his
apartment. I had my own room. Rarely
stayed the night unless it was a camping
trip. That's what Mom thought.

ACT TWO SCENE FOUR

SAM'S HOME. PAST.

SAM
    I feel like going out. Let's take a ride
    over and see where your math teacher lives.

JOHN(AGE 14)
    Ms. Teague is probably not home.

SAM
    I don't care.

JOHN(AGE 14)
    I don't know.

SAM
    Don't know what?

JOHN(AGE 14)
    Where her house is.

SAM
    I told you to find out.

JOHN(AGE 14)
    She likes me.

SAM
    Likes you? You didn't get her address
    because she likes you?

JOHN(AGE 14)
   I couldn't get it without lying to her.
   It's dishonest.

SAM
   That don't matter. You talking shit to me?
   I'm tired of whores and I want something
   clean. You best hang on to every word I'm
   about to say. You're my dog. When I say
   fetch. You fetch! Understand!

JOHN doesn't reply.

SAM
   I ain't fucking gonna wait much longer for
   an answer. I said, 'You understand dog'.

JOHN still doesn't reply.

SAM
   Look at me when I talk to you!

JOHN(AGE 14) *(defiant)*
   No. Sir.

SAM
   I'm gonna break you boy!

*SAM starts to unbuckle his belt. SAM pauses holding his belt.
JOHN turns to NANCY.*

JOHN (AGE 35)
    Mr. Henderson my math teacher used to have
    this stick he called 'stinger'. If he saw
    you nodding off in class he would slap
    'stinger' on your desk. Sometimes he would
    take us into the hallway and whip our asses
    with it. It did sting. Sam's belt left me
    black and blue. His eyes turned black.
    I've never seen him so angry. A week
    later. I had to make up for it.

ACT TWO SCENE FIVE

THE CORNER MARKET. PAST.

The week after. JOHN is in front of the store sitting on the curb searching. As SUSAN approaches the store, he grabs his knee in pain. She is a blonde with long hair.

SUSAN
   Are you okay?

JOHN(AGE 14)
   I'm fine.

SUSAN
   What happened? You cut yourself?

JOHN(AGE 14)
   It's okay.

SUSAN
   Where's your mom?

JOHN(AGE 14)
   I don't have a mom.

SUSAN
   Your dad?

JOHN (AGE 14)
    He's a cop. But he's working. I was
    riding home from school on my bike and
    these kids pushed me over.

SUSAN
    Goodness. Let me get something to clean
    this up. Surely, they have something
    inside.

SUSAN quickly gets a small first aid kit to clean up the cuts. SAM appears from around the corner. He nods his approval to JOHN. SAM steps away as SUSAN reappears.

JOHN (AGE 14)
    Thanks.

SUSAN
    This is going to hurt.

JOHN (AGE 14)
    I can take it.

SUSAN sprays antiseptic and JOHN acts like it stings.

SUSAN
    Told you it would smart.

JOHN (AGE 14)
    It will stop hurting.

SUSAN
    You are a very brave boy. Young man.

JOHN (AGE 14)
    They took my bike.

SUSAN
    The boys?

JOHN (AGE 14)
    I don't know how I am going to get home.

SUSAN
    I'll have the store clerk call your father.

JOHN (AGE 14)
    He's working.

SUSAN
    I'm sure your dad being a cop and all would
    be able to come get you under the
    circumstances.

JOHN (AGE 14)
    I don't want to bother him.

SUSAN
    Any father would not mind.

JOHN (AGE 14)
    I just want to go home.

SUSAN
    Where do you live?

JOHN (AGE 14)
    Out by the airport. On a farm.

SUSAN
    Would it make you happy if I took you home?
    What time does your dad get off work?

JOHN(AGE 14)
    Around seven.

SUSAN *(smiling)*
    Here's my car. Sorry it's dirty.

JOHN(AGE 14)
    I'll clean it for you.

SUSAN
    Your sweet. Your father raised a good boy.

JOHN(AGE 14)
    You'll like him. He adopted me. Are you
    married?

SUSAN
    No not yet. I just finished college.

JOHN(AGE 14)
    I know he's lonely and misses his wife. He
    told me likes blondes with long hair. The
    ladies at my school say he's handsome.

SUSAN
    You little matchmaker. Maybe he can help
    me with a traffic ticket for being a good
    samaritan.

JOHN(AGE 14) *(smiling at her)*
    He's gonna like you.

JOHN and SUSAN are driving in the car.

SUSAN
    Where is this place?

JOHN(AGE 14)
  We're close. Sometimes I get lost.

SUSAN
  I'm sure we will find it. Did you say
  right at the next road? There is nothing
  out here. Isn't that the airport?

JOHN(AGE 14)
  Yes. The runways are on the other side of
  that fence.

*A motorcycle cop appears behind them with the lights on and siren.
This should be sudden, loud and startling. It is SAM.*

SUSAN
  Oh shit! Sorry. I can't get another
  ticket.

She pulls over. SAM approaches the window.

SAM
  Evening Ma'am. May I see your license?

SUSAN
  Sure. What did I do?

SAM
  Ran that stop sign.

SUSAN
  What stop sign? Sorry. I didn't see it.
  I was taking this young man home and.

SAM
John? What are you doing with this lady?

SUSAN
You're his?

JOHN(AGE 14)
Hi dad.

SUSAN
Oh, thank god!

SAM
What are you doing with my son?

SUSAN
You son was at the store and he hurt
himself because some boys took his bike.
He was upset. So, I offered. He asked me
to give him a ride home. Tell him.

SAM
That was creative boy. You're good. *(to
SUSAN)* Don't you think?

SUSAN
Yes. He's a fine boy. Very polite and a
gentleman. Glad to hear that there are men
like you that will take the time to teach
your kids.

JOHN(AGE 14)
You can help her. She has tickets.

SUSAN
I'm not asking for that.

SAM
    No. Now fair is fair. You brought my boy
    home. I could overlook this.

SUSAN
    I do appreciate it. Officer.

SAM
    Sam. Call me Sam.

SUSAN
    Thanks Officer Sam.

SAM
    No. Sam.

SUSAN
    Sam.

SAM
    Here's your license. Susan. Now about the
    other tickets.

SUSAN
    Nothing really. Speeding.

SAM
    I can take care of it for you.

SUSAN
    That would be great. Not necessary. But
    great.

JOHN (AGE 14)
    Told you he could help.

SAM
    All you need to do is ask. I said ask.

SUSAN
    Okay. Would you please take care of my
    tickets?

SAM
    I afraid it's going to take a little more
    than that.

SUSAN
    I don't understand.

SAM
    We're starting to have a problem here. Get
    out of the car. Now!

*SAM opens the door. SUSAN gets out of the car. SAM pushes
against her.*

SUSAN
    Your son is in the car.

SAM
    You want those tickets taken care of?

SUSAN
    Yes. Please.

SAM
    Really?

SAM
    Boy. You stay in the car. *(to SUSAN)*
    Come with me.

SAM beats SUSAN in shadow.

JOHN (AGE 35)
    That's when the screaming started. I
    rolled up the windows on the car.

SUSAN struggles with SAM. He chokes SUSAN.

JOHN (AGE 35)
    The sun was going down. Oklahoma has such
    beautiful sunsets. I could now see the
    blue lights of the runway. I love watching
    the planes take off. I sat there wondering
    where they were going.

*SUSAN is dead. SAM takes out a knife and draws to her neck.
JOHN exits from the car. SAM hides the knife from him.*

SAM *(lovingly)*
    Come here. It's okay. Come here.

JOHN (AGE 14) *(stuttering)*
    What's wrong with her?

SAM
    She didn't love me. She's just sleeping.

JOHN (AGE 14)
    Why is she staring at me?

*NANCY enters. SAM drags SUSAN's body offstage. JOHN stares
at SAM. NANCY hugs JOHN. Tears stream down JOHN's face.*

ACT THREE SCENE ONE

NANCY'S OFFICE. NOW.

NANCY
    Dear God.

JOHN(AGE 35)
    Afterward he put me on the back of his
    motorcycle, and we rode off. The night air
    was chilly, and I was cold. I buried my
    face into his back. I remembered thinking.
    I don't remember what I was thinking. We
    stopped at a store and he bought me a hot
    chocolate and a candy bar. He. He had a
    beer and drank it very fast. We both sat
    there not saying a word. He broke the
    silence by saying "you did good kid". The
    praise that I had long for had finally
    come. It didn't feel as good as I imagined
    it would. I went home and laid awake
    watching the fish swim in my aquarium.

NANCY
    Did you comprehend?

JOHN(AGE 35)
    I know you and others think I'm stupid or
    slow.

NANCY
    I didn't mean.

JOHN (AGE 35)
   I'm smarter than you think. At an early
   age I often questioned my mother about
   Santa Claus. How could it be that twenty
   minutes ago we saw him in a different
   department store? The explanation.
   Helpers.

SAM enters wearing his biker leathers and smoking.

JOHN (AGE 35)
   That weekend we had the neighbors over for
   a sleepover to watch scary movies. That
   was the first time I had ever seen a
   Dracula movie. There was this man. His
   name was Renfield that came to visit
   Dracula. Dracula was nice to him. But
   later Renfield learned that Dracula was not
   what he seemed. Renfield eventually helped
   him. He didn't have a choice. In the
   middle of the movie I panicked. I ran out
   of the house and went outside to look at
   the stars. Don't be afraid they said.
   Telling me it was only a movie. They had
   no clue how real it was.

JOHN walks over to SAM and takes his hand.

JOHN (AGE 35)
   I now understood my role.

SAM exits.

JOHN (AGE 35)
    He wasn't always a monster. As time went
    on, he bought me things to play with at his
    apartment. Sam was very competitive and
    didn't like to lose. I didn't either. It
    was nice to be on the same playing field as
    him. Even for a moment.

ACT THREE SCENE TWO

SAM'S HOME. PAST.

SAM and JOHN are at his apartment. They are playing a video game. SAM is sitting in his chair. JOHN is at his feet.

SAM
   Five to three. Not looking good for you.

JOHN(AGE 14)
   Not done yet.

JOHN scores.

JOHN(AGE 14)
   Ha!

SAM
   Still down by one. You ain't won yet.

JOHN(AGE 14)
   Do you play tennis?

SAM
   Fuck no.

JOHN(AGE 14)
    There's a court down at the park on
    Central. I have always wanted to play.

SAM
    Basketball. I can play that.

JOHN(AGE 14)
    Are you good?

SAM
    Played some in high school. Yeah. I was
    good. Damn good.

JOHN(AGE 14)
    Can you teach me? I would love to beat
    Randy.

SAM
    Is that fucker still in your shit?

JOHN(AGE 14)
    Yes.

SAM
    I can take care of that. Nobody fucks with
    you.

JOHN(AGE 14)
    I can do it.

SAM
    Hiding in your house. Afraid to go outside
    when he's there. That don't cut it.
    That'll change. Yeah. I teach ya.

SAM scores.

SAM
    Done.

JOHN scores right behind him.

JOHN(AGE 14)
    Done!

JOHN scores.

JOHN(AGE 14)
    Again!

SAM
    You shit. One more round.

JOHN(AGE 14)
    I'll beat you again.

SAM
    Not this time. Ready.

JOHN(AGE 14)
    Go.

SAM
    You need to stand up for yourself.

JOHN(AGE 14)
    I don't want to fight him. I just want to
    beat him at basketball.

SAM
    You can do it.

JOHN (AGE 14)
    I'm not big like you. You've always been
    bigger than everyone else.

SAM
    Then you use your mind.

SAM scores.

SAM
    Ha! Pay attention. Out fox them.

JOHN (AGE 14)
    What's that?

SAM
    Be one step ahead. Think what they might
    do. Like war.

SAM scores.

SAM
    You are letting me win. I want you to
    fight.

JOHN (AGE 14)
    Why does everything have to be a fight?

SAM
    It's life.

JOHN (AGE 14)
    Do you believe in God?

SAM
   No.

JOHN (AGE 14)
   You don't think there is a heaven?

SAM
   You ask dumb questions.

JOHN (AGE 14)
   I think there is a heaven. I have a friend
   that's a Mormon.

SAM
   What's a Mormon?

JOHN (AGE 14)
   They're like Methodists except they are
   happier. Much nicer than Baptists.
   They're mean. And they cheat at
   volleyball.

SAM
   What makes them so happy?

JOHN (AGE 14)
   They have these churches called temples.
   You have to earn your way in. I guess by
   doing good things. After they come out of
   the temple, they seem so happy. Maybe they
   see God in there.

SAM
   Just a building.

JOHN (AGE 14)
   I don't want to play anymore.

SAM looks at him sternly.

JOHN (AGE 14)
    May I stop?

SAM
    Suit yourself.

SAM continues playing. JOHN picks up a book on the table. It is a scrapbook filled with pictures.

JOHN (AGE 14)
    I didn't know you keep a scrapbook. My
    Mormon friend does this too. They have
    everything. Baby pictures, ticket stubs.
    Whatever.

SAM
    Mine's the same.

JOHN (AGE 14)
    These are just pictures of women.

SAM
    My girls.

JOHN puts the book down.

SAM
    I got a question for you.

JOHN (AGE 14)
    Sure.

SAM
    Do you believe in the devil?

JOHN (AGE 14)
    Yes.

SAM
    Then do you believe that the devil has his
    own temple that you need to earn your way
    into?

JOHN (AGE 14)
    I guess so.

SAM *(SAM smiles)*
    I guess that's where you would find your
    Baptists.

JOHN doesn't know whether to laugh or not.

JOHN (AGE 14)
    When did you first meet the devil?

SAM
    Are you judging me kid?

JOHN (AGE 14)
    No. I'm just curious.

SAM
    Damn. Do you ever stop with the questions?
    I meet the devil when I was a kid.

JOHN (AGE 14)
    What did he look like?

SAM
    You want to know. Like my father. He used
    to beat me hard often for no reason. I
    think he enjoyed it. My mother couldn't
    stop it. I was so happy when that son of a
    bitch died of cancer. I liked watching him
    suffer. I really got to know the devil
    with that man. Then I went to Nam. The
    devil and I became good friends there.

JOHN (AGE 14)
    What is Nam?

SAM
    Hell. After I got home that devil moved in
    with me.

JOHN (AGE 14)
    I believe he was born a happy person then
    he fell from God's grace. I don't know
    what he did. I wish you were happy.

SAM *(coldly)*
    You've seen what makes me happy. You love
    me?

JOHN (AGE 14)
    Yes sir.

JOHN lays his head on SAM's shoulder. JOHN is comfortable there.

ACT THREE SCENE THREE

NANCY'S OFFICE. NOW.

NANCY enters. SAM remains. SAM in this scene is in JOHN's mind.

```
JOHN(AGE 35)  (To NANCY)
    He was my first.  Sam had a way of dangling
    carrots.  If I didn't deliver.  He would
    say "No wife.  Your strife."

NANCY
    You're shaking.
```

JOHN is uncomfortable with SAM in the room.

```
SAM
    You talk too much.

JOHN(AGE 35)  (to NANCY)
    I have nothing else to say.

NANCY
    What happened to him?
```

SAM snaps his fingers and JOHN reluctantly approaches him.

NANCY
    John?

JOHN(AGE 35) *(To NANCY)*
    I've said too much.

NANCY reaches for JOHN's hand.

NANCY
    You're still cutting yourself?

JOHN(AGE 35)
    No.

NANCY
    I know this is hard.

JOHN(AGE 35)
    It helps relieve stress.

SAM begins to approach JOHN.

JOHN(AGE 35)
    I'm sorry sir.

SAM
    You talk too much boy.

JOHN(AGE 35)
    It's just between me and her.

SAM
    You've always had a mouth on you.

JOHN(AGE 35)
    Please forgive me.

SAM
    That won't undo it kid.

JOHN(AGE 35)
    I'll never do it again. I'll never see her
    again.

SAM
    I know what you're doing. Trying to get
    rid of me. Let me remind you that I'm in
    you. I'm in you good.

JOHN(AGE 35)
    I'll do anything you want.

NANCY
    John?

SAM
    Ignore the bitch.

JOHN(AGE 35)
    Yes sir.

SAM
    I've always had a soft spot for you.

NANCY
    He's not real. Listen to me.

SAM
    Then show me some blood tonight. You do
    that. All is forgiven.

JOHN closes his eyes tight. His inner struggle visible on his face. SAM exits.

JOHN (AGE 35)
   I'm good. Sorry.

NANCY
   I can give you some medication to help with
   this.

JOHN (AGE 35)
   No. I just need to take a walk. This
   isn't real. None of this is real. I'm
   sorry to waist you time.

JOHN starts to leave.

NANCY
   I do believe you.

JOHN (AGE 35)
   I don't believe myself.

JOHN exits. An elderly man sits in NANCY's lobby. It is an older SAM. JOHN looks at him but does not recognize him.

SAM
   Looks like you've seen a ghost.

JOHN (AGE 35)
   Sorry.

SAM
   Is she good?

JOHN (AGE 35) *(confused)*
    Yes. Very. Have a good day.

SAM
    I lost my son.

JOHN (AGE 35)
    Sorry to hear.

SAM
    Have a good day.

JOHN exits. SAM greets NANCY.

NANCY
    Mr. Smith

SAM
    Call me Bill.

NANCY
    So, Bill. Did you ever reach out to your
    son?

SAM
    I said 'hello'. He didn't say much.

NANCY
    Understandable, considering how long it has
    been.

SAM
    I brought some pictures.

NANCY
    Your son?

SAM
    This is him at all of his school plays. I
    went to every show. Graduation. First day
    of college. His partner. You might
    recognize him.

NANCY is looking at the pictures.

NANCY
    Looks like you are proud of him.

SAM
    I'm not a dead-beat dad. I've always been
    there. Watching him.

NANCY
    This is John.

SAM
    He's a good boy. *(coldly)* But he lies.
    (smiles)

ACT THREE SCENE FOUR

THE PARK. NOW.

ABAGAIL is sitting on her bench. JOHN enters.

ABAGAIL
  Do you hear the birds singing?

JOHN (AGE 35)
  Yes.

ABAGAIL
  You know a bird wakes up every day singing.

JOHN (AGE 35)
  They're happy.

ABAGAIL
  Indeed, they are. Born happy. Dies happy.
  A bird knows he will find plenty to eat.
  Never worries about if the cat will get him
  today.

JOHN (AGE 35)
  Wish I could be that way.

ABAGAIL
  You can be. Us humans are supposed to be
  the most evolved creatures on the planet.
  Hmm.

JOHN(AGE 35)
  Good point.

ABAGAIL
  Learn from the animals.

JOHN(AGE 35)
  You seem to know. Do they think?

ABAGAIL
  Here's the answer you seek. Don't live in
  the penthouse.

ABAGAIL touches his head.

JOHN(AGE 35)
  I must think.

ABAGAIL
  Heart and mind. Find the balance.

JOHN(AGE 35)
  How?

ABAGAIL
  Don't talk to yourself. Get out of the
  conversation. I see about five or six
  voices carrying on in there. Discussing
  this and that. Simply stop it. When they
  talk to you. Don't answer. They'll go
  away. Especially that demon. Buddha calls
  him Mara. You will then find your true
  voice. One voice.

JOHN(AGE 35)
  I see.

ABAGAIL
  Mind be still. It will respond.

JOHN (AGE 35)
  I don't.

ABAGAIL
  You have time. You make time to train the
  body in your gym. Make time to train the
  mind. If you do. You will find peace.

JOHN (AGE 35)
  Peace?

ABAGAIL
  Yes. Fight for your peace.

JOHN (AGE 35)
  Is it possible?

ABAGAIL
  I see love blossoming in you.

JOHN (AGE 35)
  You see love?

ABAGAIL
  It has been so long since you have been in
  the energy of love. You don't even
  recognize it. But yet it is there.

JOHN (AGE 35)
  Who are you really?

ABAGAIL
  One who simply cares. Who are you?

JOHN (AGE 35)
  I don't know.

ABAGAIL
    You will benefit from a trip to Asia.
    Study the Buddha. You may just find
    yourself there.

JOHN (AGE 35)
    I have no plans to go.

ABAGAIL
    Your soul will make sure you get there.

JOHN (AGE 35)
    My soul?

ABAGAIL
    Hard to exist without one. Good night
    John. One more thing. You can lie to
    others. But you cannot lie to yourself.
    Always make the loving choice.

ABAGAIL walks slowly away. He looks after her.

ACT THREE SCENE FIVE

NANCY'S OFFICE. NOW.

NANCY
These are the pictures.

JOHN (AGE 35)
How long has he been seeing you?

NANCY
A month after you. Is this man your
father? I thought you said Bill was dead.

JOHN (AGE 35)
I need to think.

NANCY
About what?

JOHN (AGE 35) *(angerly)*
Give me space.

NANCY
Okay.

JOHN (AGE 35)
What did he say?

NANCY
Sorry. It's confidential.

JOHN (AGE 35)
  Seriously?

NANCY
  He wants to visit with you. Here. With
  me.

JOHN (AGE 35)
  I see.

NANCY
  Are you comfortable with that?

JOHN (AGE 35)
  No! Oh my God! That was him at the
  airport that night with Minette. And then
  later watching me in the backyard. Have
  you not been listening to me?

NANCY
  It might be good to see him. When you're
  ready.

JOHN (AGE 35)
  What is he like?

NANCY
  Pleasant enough. He seems sincere.

JOHN (AGE 35)
  Does any of this bother you?

NANCY
  I'm not sure what to think. A father
  wanting to connect with his son. In this
  way. I've seen it before. Perhaps he
  wants you to not feel threatened. Safe.

JOHN looks at her in horror. Then JOHN realizes NANCY doesn't believe what he has told her about Sam.

JOHN(AGE 35)
    He's a monster. This is his idea of a
    reunion. You, me and him. Don't you see
    it? I'll see him. But not here. Not with
    you.

NANCY
    He was insistent. "This way or no way"
    were his words. He feels bad about the
    estrangement and how it happened.

JOHN(AGE 35)
    Feels?

NANCY
    He cried.

JOHN(AGE 35)
    Set up the meeting.

ACT THREE SCENE SIX

CHRUCH COURTYARD. NOW.

JOHN is walking down the street. Looking over his shoulder. Stressed. Comes upon a statue of an angel. Looks up at it. Sits in front of it. Closes his eyes. He hears the screaming of a woman. Opens his eyes and the screaming stops. Takes a breath. Closes his eyes. Flashback begins.

JOHN(AGE 14) *(offstage voice)*
    Can you walk me to my door? Please.

DENISE *(offstage voice)*
    Sure sweetie.

JOHN(AGE 14) *(offstage voice)*
    Come on in. My dad will be home shortly.
    Maybe you can stay.

DENISE *(offstage voice)*
    I can't stay but just a minute.

JOHN(AGE 14) *(offstage voice)*
    Do you mind taking your shoes off?

DENISE *(offstage voice)*
    Of course.

JOHN(AGE 14) *(offstage voice)*
    His way or no way.

DENISE *(offstage voice)*
    What does your father do?

DENISE enters. JOHN stands. Pulls out a pair of handcuffs.

JOHN(AGE 14)
    See what he gave me.

DENISE
    I hope he is a cop.

JOHN(AGE 14)
    Not a real one.

DENISE
    Security guard?

JOHN(AGE 14)
    He's got many jobs.

SAM enters. JOHN looks over at SAM who is standing behind DENISE. JOHN smiles at him. DENISE does not notice SAM.

JOHN(AGE 14)
    Try these on.

DENISE
    I don't think so.

JOHN(AGE 14)
    Do it bitch.

SAM
　　What did you call her?

DENISE *(startled)*
　　Jesus.

SAM
　　Didn't mean to startle you. *(to JOHN)*
　　Apologize to the lady.

JOHN(AGE 14)
　　No.

SAM
　　I ain't gonna tell you again. Apologize to
　　the lady.

JOHN(AGE 14)
　　Make me.

SAM
　　You're gonna get my belt boy.

DENISE
　　Not a big deal.

JOHN(AGE 14)
　　Bitch, Bitch, Bitch.

SAM
　　I'm gonna slap some manners into you.

SAM raises his hand to JOHN.

DENISE
  Stop it please. It's okay. You don't have
  to hit him.

*DENISE comes between SAM and JOHN. SAM hits DENISE hard
in the face and knocks her down. JOHN walks over and stands over
DENISE.*

JOHN(AGE 14)
  That was meant for me.

*SAM and JOHN smile like two devils at each other. SAM is pleased
with his protégé. SAM lowers himself on top of DENISE hovering
over his prey. DENISE is semi-conscious. JOHN stands over them
watching. DENISE is pleading with SAM. JOHN continues to
watch.*

DENISE
  Not in front of the boy.

SAM
  He likes to watch me work.

*SAM seizes DENISE's throat and starts choking her. DENISE
gasps for a breath.*

DENISE *(to JOHN)*
  Help me!

SAM chokes her again.

SAM
    I'm gonna keep you. You smell nice.

DENISE
    Please!

SAM *(to DENISE)*
    Shut up! *(to JOHN)* Should I? Answer me.
    Can't take all night. You got school.
    What'll it be?

JOHN(AGE 14)
    Yes.

SAM
    Good choice.

SAM chokes DENISE taking her to near death.

SAM
    What's her name son?

JOHN(AGE 14)
    Bitch.

SAM
    Come give your Daddy a hand.

SAM takes JOHN's hand and places on her neck.

SAM
    You see this point?

```
JOHN (AGE 14)
   Yes.

SAM
   Now put your thumb and fingers like so.
   And apply some pressure.  Good.  Try it
   again.
```

JOHN pushes his fingers on DENISE's throat.

```
SAM
   Good.  Now try it again.  Harder this time.
```

DENISE chokes. JOHN jumps back.

```
SAM (comforting and lovingly)
   It's okay.  Doesn't always work the first
   time.
```

JOHN tries again. DENISE chokes.

```
SAM
   Here let me help you.
```

SAM grabs JOHN's hand and places it around DENISE's neck. Then SAM places his hand over JOHN's hand. SAM and JOHN choke her to death. DENISE struggles one last time before dying.

SAM
    Fetch me something to drink.

JOHN(AGE 14)
    I thought you said I can't open the
    refrigerator.

SAM
    You just graduated. We'll celebrate with a
    beer boy. *(singing)* A horseman rides in
    the middle of the night. Pull your covers
    up cause it's a fright. Stay in bed or you
    might be dead.

JOHN opens the door to reveal three severed women's heads in clear plastic bags. JOHN stands there in shock.

SAM *(softly)*
    Cause the horseman may come for your head.

JOHN(AGE 14) *(quietly)*
    I think. I think I want to go home. I've
    got some homework. I want my dad.

JOHN looks immediately for SAM's reaction. JOHN knows he just made a big mistake. SAM slowly approaches him.

JOHN
    I need to go. I want my daddy.

SAM
    That would be best considering your 'daddy'
    would be missing you. Like he did every...

night you've been over here. What did he
say? Tell me. What did he say?

JOHN(AGE 14)
  He wondered where I was. He asked me. I
  had to lie.

SAM
  Lie. You tell lots of lies don't you.

JOHN(AGE 14)
  You made me tell lies. I just need to go
  home.

SAM
  You are lying to me now.

JOHN(AGE 14)
  I love you.

SAM
  But you know that people who love each
  other don't just 'need to go home.'

JOHN(AGE 14)
  I'm tired.

SAM
  Don't lie to me. *(yelling)* Don't fucking
  lie to me!

JOHN(AGE 14)
  I'm not.

SAM
  Your dad don't know shit. He doesn't give
  a shit about you.

SAM takes his belt and puts around JOHN's neck and tightens it.
JOHN struggles to breathe and then SAM releases the pressure.

SAM
    My dog. Old and in so much pain. I could
    hear his cries and whimpers. I couldn't
    take it anymore. He was my only friend.

SAM tightens the belt again.

SAM
    I turned him around. I couldn't stand to
    look into his eyes. He had pretty eyes.
    Kind eyes. There was blood all over me. I
    had to do it. I loved him. He loved me.
    You don't.

JOHN(AGE 14)
    I do.

SAM
    I've fucked you up. Planted a bad seed
    deep in you.

JOHN(AGE 14)
    I love my dog too.

SAM
    He never left me.

JOHN(AGE 14)(crying)
    I'll never leave you.

SAM
    My dog.

SAM pets his head.

SAM
    Your gonna leave on my terms.

JOHN (AGE 14)
    Yes, sir.

SAM
    Close your eyes.

JOHN (AGE 14)
    Will I see Jesus?

SAM
    Yes.

JOHN (AGE 14)
    God will be happy with me?

SAM
    Yes.

JOHN (AGE 14)
    Can I look into your eyes? Please.

SAM turns him around. Tightens the belt. JOHN begins to struggle.

SAM
    I'm sorry, Bo.

JOHN (AGE 14)
    I'm sorry.

JOHN takes his finger and stabs SAM in the eye.

SAM is in pain and releases JOHN.

JOHN makes his way for the door. The door is locked. JOHN cannot escape.

SAM pauses and mends his eye. SAM walks slowly towards JOHN. SAM reaches into his pocket and pulls out a key and drops it on the floor at his feet.

JOHN cautiously approaches the key and picks it up. He hurries back to the door. He cannot put the key in the lock because his hands are shaking.

SAM helps him steady the key to unlock the door.

JOHN opens the door. Looks at SAM.

SAM slams the door shut pinning JOHN against the door. SAM puts a knife in his face.

SAM
    You betray me. I will cut you. I will
    hunt down everything you love. Get outta
    here.

SAM opens the door. JOHN exits. SAM notices a valentine card from John. He opens the card and reads it.

SAM
    Dear Sam. I love you.

SAM closes the card and walks over to his 'trophy scrapbook' and puts the card in the book along with the pictures of his victims. He sits in his chair and holds the book to his chest, arms folded.

JOHN enters and looks at SAM. JOHN is standing next to the statue.

JOHN (AGE 35) *(to the angel statue)*
    You know the truth. I know the truth. No
    one could ever believe such a story.
    What's one more lie to hide the truth?
    (yelling into the night) To thy own
    fucking self be fucking true!

ACT THREE SCENE SEVEN

NANCY'S OFFICE. NOW.

JOHN(AGE 35)
   I guess I owe you an apology.

NANCY
   How do you feel?

JOHN(AGE 35)
   To get the truth out. Stop my ridiculous
   lies about my father. A monster that never
   existed. All in my head. Who would have
   thought that slipping on ice and banging my
   head cause such trauma?

NANCY
   Yes.

JOHN(AGE 35)
   Is he coming?

NANCY
   He said he would be here.

JOHN(AGE 35)
   Maybe he decided not to.

NANCY
   I just spoke with him yesterday. You seem
   nervous.

JOHN(AGE 35)
    I've never had a poker face.

Knocking on the door.

NANCY
    The waiting is over. It's okay. Try not
    to be judgmental.

NANCY opens the door. SAM enters wearing a security guard uniform and a leather long coat.

SAM
    Morning.

NANCY
    Bill.

SAM
    Hi John.

JOHN(AGE 35)
    Hi. Bill.

NANCY
    Have a seat.

JOHN(AGE 35)
    Still riding?

SAM
    Yes. Do you?

JOHN (AGE 35)
    Have not been on a bike in years. Married?

SAM
    I wasn't very good at marriage. You
    remember. Your mother and I had our
    problems. Sorry for that. You?

JOHN (AGE 35)
    Not yet. Gay actually.

SAM
    I know.

JOHN (AGE 35)
    You seem to know a lot about me.

SAM
    I've been in touch with what's going on.

JOHN (AGE 35)
    From the shadows.

SAM
    I'm sorry for that.

JOHN (AGE 35)
    Really?

SAM
    Yes. Really. Don't get smart. Please.

JOHN (AGE 35) *(sarcastically)*
    Yes. Sir.

They stare each other down.

SAM
    He's smarter than he looks. You're not
    stuttering.

JOHN(AGE 35)
    Over the years I learned the benefits of
    biting my tongue.

SAM
    You've been good about that. Until lately.
    I may have been a little heavy handed at
    times.

JOHN(AGE 35)
    You just wanted the best for me.

SAM
    Absolutely.

JOHN(AGE 35)
    So, are you dating anyone?

SAM
    I find one now and then that's willing to
    put up with me. You gotta release stress.
    Mam. Don't mean to offend. That's guy
    talk.

JOHN(AGE 35)
    When was the last one?

SAM
    Nuff about me. Do you like your job?

JOHN(AGE 35)
    It's good.

NANCY
    Would you two like some privacy?

SAM
    This is fine. I like having you here.

JOHN(AGE 35)
    Why are you here?

SAM
    To reconnect.

JOHN(AGE 35)
    Hoping that things would be as they used to
    be. Before you left.

SAM
    We had a falling out. You're mother and
    me.

JOHN(AGE 35)
    And all this time I thought it was me.

SAM
    It wasn't about you. I loved you.

JOHN(AGE 35)
    I loved you too.

SAM
    We always enjoyed slurpys together. It was
    a treat for him.

JOHN(AGE 35)
    I remember.

SAM
    You worked hard for them.

JOHN(AGE 35)
    Gave me my first taste of beer. Very
    early.

SAM *(to NANCY)*
    He kept that secret from his mother. I
    accepted him for who he was. Even though
    he hadn't figured it out yet.

JOHN(AGE 35)
    She wouldn't have understood. Never did.
    But she was there.

SAM
    I often entertained the notion of what life
    would have been like without her in the
    way. I hope you understand.

JOHN(AGE 35)
    Perfectly.

SAM
    But you turned out well.

JOHN(AGE 35)
    Considering. I love my job and my partner.

SAM
    Still. Must bother you that you can't be
    open about that relationship.

JOHN(AGE 35)
    I respect his privacy. Always have.
    Always will.

SAM
    You have nerves of steel. He could tell
    stories. Never could talk openly about
    what was really bothering him. I used to…

tell him let people know where you are
coming from.

JOHN(AGE 35)
   I always knew where you were coming from.

SAM
   You're better for it.

JOHN(AGE 35)
   I have told stories to Nancy. Made up
   stories. Of which I deeply regret.

SAM
   I didn't mean to hurt you.

JOHN(AGE 35)
   Why did I get that consideration?

SAM
   You're my son. That's why.

JOHN(AGE 35)
   I see.

NANCY
   How do you feel John?

JOHN(AGE 35)
   I never thought I would see this day. Numb
   is how I feel.

NANCY
   That's normal.

JOHN(AGE 35)
   How do you feel. Dad?

SAM walks behind NANCY. Looks down at her. Stalking his prey.

SAM
    Outside of being lonely. I'm happy to see
    you. Talk to you.

JOHN(AGE 35)
    And.

SAM
    To build trust with you. Things have
    changed. I no longer drink. I knew it was
    a problem.

JOHN(AGE 35)
    You have changed?

SAM
    Yes. Maybe we can hang out. Get to know
    each other again.

JOHN(AGE 35)
    One afternoon to build trust?

SAM
    It's a start.

JOHN(AGE 35)
    Maybe.

SAM
    I would like to see you again. I have
    cancer.

*SAM walks over to give JOHN a hug. JOHN is not receptive.
SAM walks away.*

ACT THREE SCENE EIGHT

DINER PATIO. NOW.

SAM is sitting at a table. JOHN enters.

SAM
    Why did you keep me waiting?

JOHN (AGE 35)
    Honestly, I've been sitting in my car smoking debating on whether I wanted to see you.

SAM
    You can smoke here.

JOHN (AGE 35)
    Not that kind of smoke.

SAM
    How high are you?

JOHN (AGE 35)
    Not high enough.

SAM
    We can go back to my place.

JOHN (AGE 35)
    I'm not comfortable with that.

SAM
    In the past you couldn't wait to see me.

JOHN(AGE 35)
    Well a lot happened along the way.

SAM
    So.

JOHN(AGE 35)
    So. I don't even know what to say to you.

SAM
    Nice to see you.

JOHN(AGE 35)
    Why? I should call the police.

SAM
    I may be older, but I can still snap your
    neck in two seconds.

JOHN(AGE 35)
    Don't threaten me. Why haven't you done it
    already?

SAM
    I should. Running your mouth. Poor Nancy.
    The situation you have put her in now.

JOHN(AGE 35)
    Leave her alone. She thinks it's all a lie
    anyway.

SAM
    You did well.

JOHN(AGE 35)
    You were at my graduation? College too?

SAM
    I've always been your guardian angel.
    Protecting you.

JOHN (AGE 35)
    From you.

SAM
    Do you miss it?

JOHN (AGE 35)
    It?

SAM
    It seemed to me that you were getting used
    to it. Enjoyed it.

JOHN (AGE 35)
    I have to now look at myself in the mirror
    every morning for the rest of my life. God
    rest their souls.

SAM
    Do you miss me?

JOHN (AGE 35)
    I idolized you. Loved you. Always wanted
    to be near you. This is going to sound
    very selfish of me considering. Why did
    you hurt me?

SAM
    This wasn't about love.

JOHN (AGE 35)
    Really? Really? Fuck you. Fuck you!

SAM
    Keep your voice down.

JOHN (AGE 35)
    It was to me. You would always go on about
    all the people in your life that fucked you
    over. Pissed on you. Right under your own
    fucking nose was someone that loved you.
    Did whatever you wanted. But that wasn't
    good enough. Why did you have to hate and
    constantly hurt the only person on this
    earth that loved you for you? And only as
    a child can do, constantly forgive you.

SAM
    Are you finished?

JOHN (AGE 35)
    No. Yes. I'm done.

SAM
    Well said. I am a broken man.

JOHN (AGE 35)
    It took cancer and facing death yourself to
    bring you to this point. Why did you
    approach me now? Fear of me spilling the
    beans?

SAM
    No. I'm good at what I do.

JOHN (AGE 35)
    I don't want to know how many more there
    are.

SAM
    You don't have to.

JOHN (AGE 35)
    Are you afraid to die?

SAM
    Yes. But I want you to do it. That's why
    I was asking if you missed it. It will
    help you get over me.

JOHN(AGE 35)
    Please don't try to manipulate me. No.
    You need to face death the way it is
    supposed to happen. Not by my hands. But
    by God.

SAM
    Will you at least help me face it?

JOHN(AGE 35)
    The secrets we keep.

SAM
    You still have the prettiest eyes that I've
    ever seen.

JOHN(AGE 35)
    I'm not a child anymore. You can't seduce
    me. Can I bum a smoke?

SAM lights JOHN's cigarette and then his. They look at each other.

JOHN(AGE 35)
    It's so strange to look at you through the
    eyes of an adult.

SAM
    That's my bike. You want to take a ride.

JOHN(AGE 35)
    Not tonight. I want to go back to my car.
    Smoke another joint. And wonder what the
    rest of my life would have been like if I
    had just stayed home tonight. I'm so
    tired.

JOHN leans over and lays on SAM's chest. SAM rubs his head gently. JOHN gets up slowly.

JOHN(AGE 35)
    Thanks for the smoke.

SAM
    I got the tab.

JOHN(AGE 35)
    Goodnight.

SAM
    John.

JOHN and SAM look at each other. SAM wants to speak but can't bring himself to say what he wants to.

JOHN(AGE 35)
    I know you do.

ACT THREE SCENE NINE

THE PARK. NOW.

SAM and JOHN are walking in the park talking.

NANCY (to audience)
    Page two hundred and twelve. I do not know
    anything about forgiveness. But overtime I
    began to feel love again. I think I
    understand love. We spent time together.
    Sam cried a lot. Sam grew sicker.

*ABAGAIL enters. Hands JOHN an apple. Touches SAM on the
face. ABAGAIL exits with SAM.*

NANCY
    We had to say goodbye. I did love that man
    that nobody could love. Abagail was right
    about bringing that ugly side of self to
    the light. His hate taught me about love.
    Most importantly self-love.

*SEAN enters dressed in a black tuxedo coat with his sports jersey
underneath.*

SEAN
    Are you ready?

JOHN(AGE 45)
    Are you?

SEAN hands him a white tuxedo coat.

JOHN(AGE 45)
    White?

SEAN
    You are a saint to me.

JOHN(AGE 45)
    Let's do this.

SEAN
    Now. Between me and you.

JOHN(AGE 45)
    Okay.

SEAN
    I Sean take you to be my lawful wedded
    husband. In sickness and in health. For
    richer or poorer. Till death do us part.

JOHN(AGE 45)
    I John take you to be my lawful wedded
    husband. In sickness and in health. For
    richer or poorer. Till death do us part.

SEAN
    You know your life will never be the same
    again as soon as we step through that door.

JOHN (AGE 45)
    Neither will yours.

SEAN
    Can you handle being a 'trophy wife'?

JOHN (AGE 45)
    Whatever.

JOHN and SEAN open door to the flash of cameras and reporters. Stage transforms to Buddhist temple in Asia. JOHN enters and sits center stage to meditate.

NANCY *(to audience)*
    Sean had to play a game in Japan. After
    some tours with the players' wives I
    decided to stay over a few weeks. I
    learned a lot. Sitting in the silence.
    Observing my thoughts and mind was like
    watching a movie. Not part of it anymore.
    Abagail was right on so many levels.

Stage transforms to the cemetery as in Act One. Scene One.

NANCY *(to audience)*
    Near Sam's grave grew a new apple tree.
    Finally, I woke up happy today.

THE END

REFERENCES

"Book of Mormon, 1830," p. 143, The Joseph
Smith Papers Online
https://www.josephsmithpapers.org/paper-
summary/book-of-mormon-1830/149
(accessed June 29, 2020)

"The Legend of Sleepy Hollow" by Washington
Irving

Bible," The Lord's Prayer", Bible. United
Methodist Version.
Online, http://www.dumc.org/the-lords-prayer
(accessed 20 May 2020)